W9-AJU-079

A long time ago, in a beautiful, quiet village on the slopes of the Mountain of Mountains, there lived a boy named Hasan. He was strong, adventurous, and courageous. The people of the village nicknamed him "Hasan the Brave."

But there was one thing that disturbed the peace in this quiet village...
Something that made the villagers live in constant fear...
It was a scary, ugly ghoul that lived in a cave at the top of the mountain.

The people of the village would tiptoe to their fields, always carefully
looking around them. They would whisper to each other,

"Good morning, neighbor. How are you? How are the children?
Inshallah, everything is good."

And whenever the children made the slightest noise while playing, their parents would say to them, "SHHHHHHHHHHHHHHHHHHHHHHHHHHHHHHHHHHHHHH! Lower your voices so that you do not disturb the ghoul."

And whenever the children laughed loudly, the old folk in the
village would say to them,
"SHHHHHHHHHHHHHHHHHHHHHHHHHHHHHHHHHHHHHHHH!
Do not laugh. Smile only so that you do not disturb the ghoul."

One day during the olive harvest, Hasan asked his aunt: "Why is it that all the people in the village are afraid of the ghoul?"

She answered in a terrified voice, "The ghoul is a huge animal. His body is covered with thick hair. He has one big eye in the middle of his forehead, and he has long claws and sharp teeth. His favorite food is little boys and girls."

But Hasan was not satisfied with this answer. When he got back home, he asked his father: "Baba, did the ghoul ever hurt anyone in the village?"

His father scratched his head and said, "No, I've never heard of anyone being hurt by the ghoul. But I know that he is scary and dangerous. God help anyone who becomes his prey."

Hasan then asked his mother: "Mama, did the ghoul ever eat any boys and girls from our village?"

She answered, "No, the ghoul did not eat any children from the village. But I heard that he is fierce. He has a voice as deep and frightening as a wolf's, and he is as strong as a lion! Swear to me that you will be careful not to disturb the ghoul."

Hasan was tired of being scared all the time so he said, "I am tired of tiptoeing around the village and of all the shushing up. I want to jump and shout and scream and laugh and climb the mountain too!

Tomorrow, bright and early, I will start my journey up the mountain. After all, I am Hasan the Brave and I will not let anyone stop me."

Umm Hasan cried and pleaded with him: "Please, Hasan, I beg you my son, do not go. I'm afraid that the ghoul will eat you."

Hasan's father pleaded with him too and asked him not to go. But Hasan had made up his mind.

Finally, Hasan arrived at the top of the mountain.
He looked around carefully, but he found nothing that
scared him.

What a spectacular view from the top of the mountain!
And how all the houses in the village looked so small!

Hasan raised both his arms and shouted as loud as he could:

"I am Hasan the Brave!
Hasan the Fearless!
I won't be afraid of the ghoul!
Never, never, never..."

Suddenly, Hasan heard a sound coming from behind him…
a sound of giant footsteps. He quickly turned around and
found himself face to face with the ghoul.

The ghoul looked exactly the way the people of the village
had described him. He was scary, with thick hair, long claws,
and one eye in the middle of his forehead.

Hasan froze in fear. He wished he had listened to everyone's
warnings and never left the village.

The ghoul came closer and closer to Hasan and crept slowly around him in a circle…

Then the ghoul ran away as fast as his legs could go.

Hasan took a deep breath. He could not believe that the huge ghoul was afraid of him—the same ghoul who had caused so much fear in the people of his village. Hasan followed the ghoul to his cave and started calling: "Ghoul, ghoul, where are you?"

The ghoul shouted back as he trembled in his cave: "Go away from here, young boy! I did not cause you any harm."

Hasan replied, "But you are the ghoul. And everyone is scared of you."

The ghoul scratched his head and said, "That is really strange! The people are afraid of me, and I am afraid of them."

Hasan laughed hard and said, "Why are you afraid of the people? You are the ghoul."

The ghoul relaxed a bit and answered, "The people look really scary. They have two eyes instead of one."

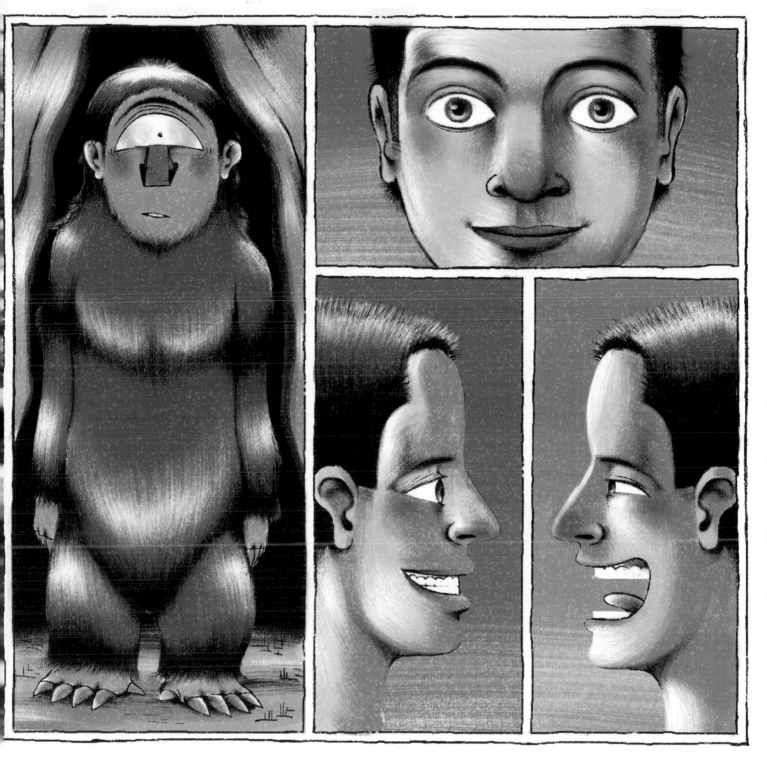

"They do not have thick hair like mine, they have strange voices, and their teeth are small, unlike mine. But most important of all, they eat ghouls."

Hasan smiled and said: "That's impossible! We don't eat ghouls. It is the ghouls that eat people."

The ghoul shook his head and said, "But… ghouls are vegetarians."

Hasan, by now totally relaxed, told the ghoul: "The people of my village are going to be very happy when I tell them this."

The ghoul took a long, hard look at Hasan and said: "It is true that you look strange and different, but you are nice." They both laughed and went off to play together.

And from that day on, the ghoul became Hasan's best friend, and was loved by the people of the village.

The story of Hasan and the ghoul was passed down through generations and reminded the villagers to celebrate their differences and never let fear rule them again.